THE SUNSET MAKER

Donald Justice

THE SUNSET MAKER

POEMS / STORIES / A MEMOIR

ATHENEUM

New York

1987

Grateful acknowledgment is made to the following magazines in which these poems and stories earlier appeared, often in provisional versions and under different titles.

AMERICAN POETRY REVIEW: *In Memory of My Friend, the Bassoonist, John Lenox*

ANTAEUS: *Mule Team and Poster*; *Lines at the New Year*; *Piano Lessons: Notes on a Provincial Culture*; *In Memory of the Unknown Poet, Robert Boardman Vaughn*; *Nostalgia of the Lakefronts*; *Cinema and Ballad of the Great Depression*; *The Artificial Moonlight*

ANTIOCH REVIEW: *Seawind: A Song*

THE ATLANTIC: *Cemetery* (from *My South*); *Epilogue: Coronado Beach, California* (from *American Scenes* [*1904–1905*]); *Mrs. Snow*

THE GRAMERCY REVIEW: *Nostalgia and Complaint of the Grandparents*

THE IOWA REVIEW: *The Sunset Maker*

MEMPHIS STATE REVIEW: *Nineteenth Century Portrait*

THE NATION: *October: A Song*; *Last Evening*; *Purgatory*; *Manhattan Dawn (1945)*

THE NEW CRITERION: *Children Walking Home from School through Good Neighborhood*; *Villanelle at Sundown*; *American Scenes (1904–1905)*, except the epilogue; *The Piano Teachers: A Memoir of the Thirties*; *Psalm and Lament*; *Afterschool Practice: An Episode*

THE NEW YORKER: *Tremayne*; *Train* (from *My South*); *The Pupil*

THE NORTH AMERICAN REVIEW: *Little Elegy for Cello and Piano*

PLOUGHSHARES: *Farm* (from *My South*)

SEQUOIA: *Young Girls Growing Up (1911)*

Several of the poems also appeared in England, in THE LONDON MAGAZINE, QUARTO, and POETRY NOW.

To the memory of my teachers

KATE HEALY SNOW   CARL RUGGLES

ROBERT BOARDMAN VAUGHN   JOHN BERRYMAN

Sec et musclé   D. MILHAUD
Avec une élégance grave et lente   C. DEBUSSY
broadly singing   C. RUGGLES

Contents

THE SUNSET MAKER

Lines at the New Year

1

The old year slips past
          unseen, the way a snake goes.
Vanishes,
          and the grass closes behind it.

2

No clouds—and the grayblues
          subside into saffron.
Delicately they subside,
          into the saffron.

Mule Team and Poster

Two mules stand waiting in front of the brick wall of a warehouse,
      hitched to a shabby flatbed wagon.
Its spoked wheels resemble crude wooden flowers
      pulled recently from a deep and stubborn mud.

The rains have passed over for now
      and the sun is back,
Invisible, but everywhere present,
      and of a special brightness, like God.

The way the poster for the traveling show
      still clings to its section of the wall
It looks as though a huge door stood open
      or a terrible flap of brain had been peeled back, revealing

Someone's idea of heaven:
      seven dancing-girls, caught on the upkick,
All in fringed dresses and bobbed hair.
      One wears a Spanish comb and has an escort . . .

Meanwhile the mules crunch patiently the few cornshucks
      someone has thoughtfully scattered for them.
The poster is torn in places, slightly crumpled;
      a few bricks, here and there, show through.

And a long shadow—
      the last shade perhaps in all of Alabama—
Stretches beneath the wagon, crookedly,
      like a great scythe laid down there and forgotten.

on a photograph by Walker Evans (Alabama, 1936)

My South

I dont! I dont hate it! I dont hate it!

Q. COMPSON

*But why do I write of the all unutterable
and the all abysmal? Why does my pen not
drop from my hand on approaching the in-
finite pity and tragedy of all the past? It
does, poor helpless pen, with what it meets
of the ineffable, what it meets of the cold
Medusa-face of life, of all the life* lived, *on
every side.* Basta, basta!

H. JAMES

1   CEMETERY

Above the fenceflowers, like a bloody thumb,
A hummingbird is throbbing. . . . And some
Petals take motion from the beaten wings
In hardly observable obscure quiverings.
My mother stands there, but so still her clothing
Seems to have settled into stone, nothing
To animate her face, nothing to read there—
O plastic rose O clouds O still cedar!
She stands this way for a long time while the sky
Ponders her with its great Medusa eye;
Or in my memory she does.
                              And then a
Slow blacksnake, lazy with long sunning, slides
Down from its slab, and through the thick grass, and hides
Somewhere among the purpling wild verbena.

5

2 FARM

And I, missing the city intensely at this moment,
Mope and sulk at the window. There's the first owl now, quite near,
But the sound hardly registers. And the kerosene lamp
Goes on sputtering, giving off vague medicinal fumes
That make me think of sickrooms. I have been memorizing
"The Ballad of Reading Gaol," but the lamplight hurts my eyes;
And I am too bored to sleep, restless and bored.

                                        Years later,
Perhaps, I will recall the evenings, empty and vast, when
Under the first stars, there by the back gate, secretly, I
Would relieve myself on the shamed and drooping hollyhocks.
Now I yawn; the old dream of being a changeling returns.
The owl cries, and I feel myself like the owl—alone, proud,
Almost invisible—or like some hero in Homer
Protected by the cloud let down by the gods to save me.

3 TRAIN

> *(Heading north through Florida, late at night and long ago,
> and ending with a line from Thomas Wolfe)*

Midnight or after, and the little lights
Glitter like lost beads from a broken necklace
Beyond smudged windows, lost and irretrievable—
Some promise of romance these Southern nights
Never entirely keep—unless, sleepless,
We should pass down dim corridors again
To stand, braced in a swaying vestibule,
Alone with the darkness and the wind—out there
Nothing but pines and one new road perhaps,
Straight and white, aimed at the distant gulf—
And hear, from the smoking room, the sudden high-pitched
Whinny of laughter pass from throat to throat;
And the great wheels smash and pound beneath our feet.

American Scenes (1904–1905)

1 CAMBRIDGE IN WINTER

Immense pale houses! Sunshine just now and snow
Light up and pauperize the whole brave show—
Each fanlight, each veranda, each good address,
All a mere paint and pasteboard paltriness!

These winter sunsets are the one fine thing:
Blood on the snow, one last impassioned fling,
The wild frankness and sadness of surrender—
As if our cities ever could be tender!

2 RAILWAY JUNCTION SOUTH OF RICHMOND, PAST MIDNIGHT

Indistinguishable engines hooting, red
Fires flaring, vanishing; a formless shed
Just straggling lifewards before sinking back
Into Dantean glooms beside the track,

All steam and smoke and earth—and even here,
Out of this little hell of spurts and hisses,
Come the first waftings of the Southern air,
Of open gates, of all but bland abysses.

3 ST. MICHAEL'S CEMETERY, CHARLESTON

One may depend on these old cemeteries
To say the one charmed thing there is to say—
As here the silvery seaward outlook carries
Hints of some other world beyond the bay,

The sun-warmed tombs, the flowers. Each faraway
Game-haunted inlet and reed-smothered isle
Speaks of lost Venices; and the South meanwhile
Has only to be tragic to beguile.

4 EPILOGUE: CORONADO BEACH, CALIFORNIA

In a hotel room by the sea, the Master
Sits brooding on the continent he has crossed.
Not that he foresees immediate disaster,
Only a sort of freshness being lost—
Or should he go on calling it Innocence?
The sad-faced monsters of the plains are gone;
Wall Street controls the wilderness. There's an immense
Novel in all this waiting to be done,
But not, not—sadly enough—by him. His talents,
Such as they may be, want an older theme,
One rather more civilized than this, on balance.
For him now always the consoling dream
Is just the mild dear light of Lamb House falling
Beautifully down the pages of his calling.

after Henry James

Nineteenth Century Portrait

Under skies God Himself must have painted blue
You came with your basket from the marketplace,
Bananas and a few ripe pineapples in it for the Boss.

Your skirt, all scarlet, and swinging with each step,
Was like the bright cape matadors show the bull;
The same cloth wound about your forehead, a richly bled bandage.

The morning of the world sat in its palm branch,
A just escaped parrot. Big mosquitoes hummed.
White men smoked on their verandas, each safe in his own small cloud.

And I imagine the straw mat you woke from;
Your dreams, too, all hummingbirds and hibiscus;
And everything I imagine is like you, simple and fresh.

I think you must have wanted to see the States,
And even then our cities were too crowded.
Down by the docks, in winter, the cold fogs could not have hidden

The truth from you very long. Fate was the rags
You stood shivering in, under the lampposts,
Above which must have risen, sometimes, tall ghosts of absent palms.

after Baudelaire

9

Young Girls Growing Up (1911)

No longer do they part and scatter so hopelessly before you,
But they will stop and put an elbow casually
On the piano top and look quite frankly at you;
And pale reflections glide there then like swans.

What you say to them now is not lost. They listen to the end
And—little heartshaped chins uplifted—seem
Just on the point of breaking into song;
Nor is a short conversation more than they can stand.

When they turn away now they do so slowly, and mean no harm;
And it seems their backs are suddenly broader also.
You picture yourself in the avenue below, masked by trees,
And, just as the streetlamps go on, you glance up:

There, there at the window, blotting out the light. . . !
Weeks pass and perhaps you meet unexpectedly,
And now they come forward mournfully, hands outstretched,
Asking why you are such a stranger, what has changed?

But when you seek them out, they only
Crouch in a window seat and pretend to read,
And have no look to spare you, and seem cruel.
And this is why there are men who wander aimlessly through cities!

This is why there are cities and darkness and a river,
And men who stride along the embankment now, without a plan,
And turn their collars up against the moon,
Saying to one another, *Live, we must try to live, my friend!*

after Kafka

10

Children Walking Home from School
through Good Neighborhood

They are like figures held in some glass ball,
One of those in which, when shaken, snowstorms occur;
But this one is not yet shaken.
        And they go unaccompanied still,
Out along this walkway between two worlds,
This almost swaying bridge.
        October sunlight checkers their path;
It frets their cheeks and bare arms now with shadow
Almost too pure to signify itself.
And they progress slowly, somewhat lingeringly,
Independent, yet moving all together,
Like polyphonic voices that crisscross
In short-lived harmonies.

        Today, a few stragglers.
One, a girl, stands there with hands spaced out, so—
A gesture in a story. Someone's school notebook spills,
And they bend down to gather up the loose pages.
(Bright sweaters knotted at the waist; solemn expressions.)
Not that they would shrink or hold back from what may come,
For now they all at once run to meet it, a little swirl of colors,
Like the leaves already blazing and falling farther north.

October: A Song

Summer, goodbye.
The days grow shorter.
Cranes walk the fairway now
In careless order.

They step so gradually
Toward the distant green
They might be brushstrokes
Animating a screen.

Mists canopy
The water hazard.
Nearby, a little flag
Lifts, brave but frazzled.

Under sad clouds
Two white-capped golfers
Stand looking off, dreamy and strange,
Like young girls in Balthus.

Seawind: A Song

Seawind, you rise
From the night waves below,
Not that we see you come and go,
But as the blind know things we know
And feel you on our face,
And all you are
Or ever were is space,
Seawind, come from so far,
To fill us with this restlessness
That will outlast your own—
So the figtree,
When you are gone,
Seawind, still bends and leans out toward the sea
And goes on blossoming alone.

after Rilke

Last Evening

And night and far to go—
For hours the convoys had rolled by
Like storm clouds in a troubled sky;
   He'd gone on playing, though,

And raised his eyes to hers,
Which had become his mirror now,
So filled were they with his clenched brow,
   And the pain to come, or worse;

And then the image blurred.
She stood at the window in the gloom
And looked back through the fading room—
   Outside, a fresh wind stirred—

And noticed across a chair
The officer's jacket he had flung
There earlier; and now it hung
   Like the coats scarecrows wear

And which the birdshadows flee and scatter from;
Or like the skin of some great battle-drum.

after Rilke

Psalm and Lament

in memory of my mother (1897–1974)
Hialeah, Florida

The clocks are sorry, the clocks are very sad.
One stops, one goes on striking the wrong hours.

And the grass burns terribly in the sun,
The grass turns yellow secretly at the roots.

Now suddenly the yard chairs look empty, the sky looks empty,
The sky looks vast and empty.

Out on Red Road the traffic continues; everything continues.
Nor does memory sleep; it goes on.

Out spring the butterflies of recollection,
And I think that for the first time I understand

The beautiful ordinary light of this patio
And even perhaps the dark rich earth of a heart.

(The bedclothes, they say, had been pulled down.
I will not describe it. I do not want to describe it.

No, but the sheets were drenched and twisted.
They were the very handkerchiefs of grief.)

Let summer come now with its schoolboy trumpets and fountains.
But the years are gone, the years are finally over.

And there is only
This long desolation of flower-bordered sidewalks

That runs to the corner, turns, and goes on,
That disappears and goes on

Into the black oblivion of a neighborhood and a world
Without billboards or yesterdays.

Sometimes a sad moon comes and waters the roof tiles.
But the years are gone. There are no more years.

In Memory of My Friend, the Bassoonist, John Lenox

1

One winter he was the best
Contrabassoonist south
Of Washington, D.C.—
The only one. Lonely

In eminence he sat,
Like some lost island king,
High on a second-story porch
Overlooking the bay

(His blue front lawn, his kingdom)
And presided over the Shakespearean
Feuds and passions of the eave-pigeons.
Who, during the missile crisis,

Had stocked his boat with booze,
Charts, and the silver flute
He taught himself to play,
Casually, one evening.

And taught himself to see,
Sailing thick glasses out blindly
Over some lily-choked canal.
O autodidact supreme!

2

John, where you are now can you see?
Do the pigeons there bicker like ours?
Does the deep bassoon not moan
Or the flute sigh ever?

No one could think it was you,
Slumped there on the sofa, despairing,
The hideous green sofa.
No, you are off somewhere,

Off with Gauguin and Christian
Amid hibiscus'd isles,
Red-mustached, pink-bearded
Again, as in early manhood.

It is well. Shark waters
Never did faze you half so much
As the terrible radios
And booboiseries of the neighbors.

Here, if you care, the bay
Is printed with many boats now,
Thick as trash; that high porch is gone,
Gone up in the smoke of money, money;

The barbarians . . .
                    But enough.
You are missed. Across the way,
Someone is practicing sonatas,
And the sea air smells again of good gin.

Coconut Grove

In Memory of the Unknown Poet,
Robert Boardman Vaughn

> *But the essential advantage for a poet is*
> *not, to have a beautiful world with which*
> *to deal: it is to be able to see beneath both*
> *beauty and ugliness; to see the boredom,*
> *and the horror, and the glory.*
>
> T. S. ELIOT

It was his story. It would always be his story.
It followed him; it overtook him finally—
The boredom, and the horror, and the glory.

Probably at the end he was not yet sorry,
Even as the boots were brutalizing him in the alley.
It was his story. It would always be his story,

Blown on a blue horn, full of sound and fury,
But signifying, O signifying magnificently
The boredom, and the horror, and the glory.

I picture the snow as falling without hurry
To cover the cobbles and the toppled ashcans completely.
It was his story. It would always be his story.

Lately he had wandered between St. Mark's Place and the Bowery,
Already half a spirit, mumbling and muttering sadly.
O the boredom, and the horror, and the glory!

All done now. But I remember the fiery
Hypnotic eye and the raised voice blazing with poetry.
It was his story and would always be his story—
The boredom, and the horror, and the glory.

Purgatory

RBV speaks: "After so many years of pursuing the ideal,
I came home. But I had caught sight of it.
You see it sometimes in the bluesilver wake
Of island schooners, bound for Anegada, say.
And it takes other forms. I saw it flickering once
In torches by the railroad tracks in Medellín.
When I was very young I thought that love would come
And seize and take me south and I would see the rose;
And that all ambiguities we knew would merge
Like orchids on a word. Say this:
I sought the immortal word."
                              So saying he went on
To join those who preceded him;
                              and there were those that followed.

Villanelle at Sundown

Turn your head. Look. The light is turning yellow.
The river seems enriched thereby, not to say deepened.
    Why this is, I'll never be able to tell you.

Or are Americans half in love with failure?
One used to say so, reading Fitzgerald, as it happened.
    (That Viking Portable, all water-spotted and yellow—

Remember?) Or does mere distance lend a value
To things?—false, it may be, but the view is hardly cheapened.
    Why this is, I'll never be able to tell you.

The smoke, those tiny cars, the whole urban milieu—
One can like *any*thing diminishment has sharpened.
    Our painter friend, Lang, might show the whole thing yellow

And not be much off. It's nuance that counts, not color—
As in some late James novel, saved up for the long weekend,
    And vivid with all the Master simply won't tell you.

How frail our generation has got, how sallow
And pinched with just surviving! We all go off the deep end
    Finally, gold beaten thinly out to yellow.
    And why this is, I'll never be able to tell you.

Nostalgia and Complaint of the Grandparents

Les morts
C'est sous terre;
Ça n'en sort
Guère.

J. LAFORGUE

Our diaries squatted, toadlike,
On dark closet ledges.
Forget-me-not and thistle
Decalcomaned the pages.
But where, where are they now,
    All the sad squalors
Of those between-wars parlors?—
Cut flowers; and the sunlight spilt like soda
    On torporous rugs; the photo
Albums all outspread . . .
    The dead
Don't get around much anymore.

There was an hour when daughters
Practiced arpeggios;
Their mothers, awkward and proud,
Would listen, smoothing their hose—
Sundays, half past five!
    Do you recall
How the sun used to loll,
Lazily, just beyond the roof,
    Bloodshot and aloof?
We thought it would never set.
    The dead don't get
Around much anymore.

Eternity resembles
One long Sunday afternoon.
No traffic passes; the cigar smoke
Coils in a blue cocoon.
Children, have you nothing
    For our cold sakes?
No tea? No little tea cakes?

Sometimes now the rains disturb
  Even our remote suburb.
  There's a dampness underground.
  The dead don't get around
    Much anymore.

Cinema and Ballad of the Great Depression

We men had kept our dignity;
Each wore a cap or a hat. It seemed
We had become a line somehow;
Dark soup was all our dream.

We moved back in with parents. Some days
The awnings creaked like sails.
We lay on the bedclothes smoking, smoking
The long afternoons away.

Sometimes, folding the evening paper up,
One feels suddenly alone.
Yes. And down the tracks at night
The slow smoke of nomad fires . . .

We slept; and over us a bridge
Arc'd like a promise. To the west
Nightglow of cities always then;
And somebody pulled out a harp.

Pulled a mouthharp out and played,
O lost and wordless . . .
And we were as numerous as leaves;
And some of us turned yellow, and some red.

Agriculture embraced Industry,
Mammothly, on public walls.
Meanwhile we camped beneath the great
Smiles on billboards fading.

And home might be some town we passed—
The gingerbread of porches scrolled
In shadow down the white housefronts;
And townboys playing baseball in a road.

Things will go better one day, boys.
Don't ask when.
A decade hence, a war away.
O meet me in the Red Star Mission then!

Pulled out an ancient mouthharp and began to play.

Manhattan Dawn (1945)

There is a smoke of memory
That curls about these chimneys
And then uncurls; that lifts,
Diaphanous, from sleep

To lead you down some alleyway perhaps
Still vaguely riverwards;
And so at length disperses
Into the wisps and tatters

That garland fire escapes.
  And you will find yourself again
Watching, beside a misty platform,
The first trucks idling to unload

(New England's frost still
Unstippling down their sides).
                  Or turn
To catch blue truant eyes upon you
Through steam that rises suddenly from a grate:

"There's no city like it in the world, son,
For sidewalk nights"—grinning;
And the grin slides off across the storefronts.
Dawn overtakes him, though,

Down Hudson somewhere, or Horatio—
  And you have seen it bend
The long stripes of the awnings down
Toward gutters whose discarded flowers

Lie washing in the night's small rain—
Hints, glimmerings of a world
Not ours.
          And office towers
Coast among lost stars.

Nostalgia of the Lakefronts

Cities burn behind us; the lake glitters.
A tall loudspeaker is announcing prizes;
Another, by the lake, the times of cruises.
Childhood, once vast with terrors and surprises,
Is fading to a landscape deep with distance—
And always the sad piano in the distance,

Faintly in the distance, a ghostly tinkling
(O indecipherable blurred harmonies)
Or some far horn repeating over water
Its high lost note, cut loose from all harmonies.
At such times, wakeful, a child will dream the world,
And this is the world we run to from the world.

Or the two worlds come together and are one
On dark sweet afternoons of storm and of rain,
And stereopticons brought out and dusted,
Stacks of old *Geographics*, or, through the rain,
A mad wet dash to the local movie palace
And the shriek, perhaps, of Kane's white cockatoo.
(Would this have been summer, 1942?)

By June the city seems to grow neurotic.
But lakes are good all summer for reflection,
And ours is famed among painters for its blues,
Yet not entirely sad, upon reflection.
Why sad at all? Is their wish not unique—
To anthropomorphize the inanimate
With a love that masquerades as pure technique?

O art and the child are innocent together!
But landscapes grow abstract, like aging parents;
Soon now the war will shutter the grand hotels;
And we, when we come back, must come as parents.
There are no lanterns now strung between pines—
Only, like history, the stark bare northern pines.

And after a time the lakefront disappears
Into the stubborn verses of its exiles
Or a few gifted sketches of old piers.
It rains perhaps on the other side of the heart;
Then we remember, whether we would or no.
—Nostalgia comes with the smell of rain, you know.

Tremayne

1 THE MILD DESPAIR OF TREMAYNE

Snow melting and the dog
Barks lonely on his bottom from the yard.
    The ground is frozen but not hard.

The seasonal and vague
Despairs of February settle over
    Tremayne now like a light snow cover,

And he sits thinking; sits
Also not thinking for a while of much.
    So February turns to March.

Snow turns to rain; a hya-
cinth pokes up; doves returning moan and sing.
    Tremayne takes note of one more spring—

Mordancies of the armchair!—
And finds it hard not to be reconciled
    To a despair that seems so mild.

2 THE CONTENTMENT OF TREMAYNE

Tremayne stands in the sunlight,
    Watering his lawn.
The sun seems not to move at all,
    Till it has moved on.

The twilight sounds commence now,
    As those of water cease,
And he goes barefoot through the stir,
    Almost at peace.

Light leans in pale rectangles
    Out against the night.
Tremayne asks nothing more now. There's
    Just enough light,

Or when the street lamp catches
    There should be. He pauses:
How simple it all seems for once!—
    These sidewalks, these still houses.

3 THE INSOMNIA OF TREMAYNE

The all-night stations—Tremayne pictures them
As towers that shoot great sparks off through the dark—
Fade out and drift among the drifted hours
Just now returning to his bedside clock;
And something starts all over, call it day.
He likes, he really likes the little hum,
Which is the last sound of all nightsounds to decay.

Call that the static of the spheres, a sound
Of pure inbetweenness, far, and choked, and thin.
As long as it lasts—a faint, celestial surf—
He feels no need to dial the weather in,
Or music, or the news, or anything.
And it soothes him, like some night-murmuring nurse,
Murmuring nothing much perhaps, but murmuring.

4 TREMAYNE AUTUMNAL

Autumn, and a cold rain, and mist,
In which the dark pineshapes are drowned,
And taller poleshapes, and the town lights masked—
A scene, oh, vaguely Post-Impressionist,
Tremayne would tell us, if we asked.

Who with his glasses off, half-blind,
Accomplishes very much the same
Lovely effect of blurs and shimmerings—
Or else October evenings spill a kind
Of Lethe-water over things.

"O season of half forgetfulness!"
Tremayne, as usual, misquotes,
Recalling adolescence and old trees
In whose shade once he memorized that verse
And something about "late flowers for the bees . . . "

Mrs. Snow

Busts of the great composers glimmered in niches,
Pale stars. Poor Mrs. Snow, who could forget her,
Calling the time out in that hushed falsetto?
(How early we begin to grasp what kitsch is!)
But when she loomed above us like an alp,
We little towns below would feel her shadow.
Somehow her nods of approval seemed to matter
More than the stray flakes drifting from her scalp.
Her etchings of ruins, her mass-production Mings
Were our first culture: she put us in awe of things.
And once, with her help, I composed a waltz,
Too innocent to be completely false
Perhaps, but full of marvellous clichés.
She beamed and softened then.

                        Ah, those were the days.

Piano Lessons: Notes on a Provincial Culture

So now it is vain for the singer to burst into clamour
With the great black piano appassionato. The glamour
Of childish days is upon me . . .

D. H. LAWRENCE

A piano lesson in those days cost fifty cents and lasted for half an hour. At that price my parents, though far from well off, were able to afford a weekly lesson for me all through the depression years. I think I guessed even then how much the lessons represented an ambition for gentility on my mother's part. Mother had studied piano herself years before and could still play certain favored hymns with a noisy and happy confidence. In bourgeois life it is the mother to whom the child's first cultural or artistic stirrings and strivings can normally be traced, and this was certainly true of my own history.

Sometimes the half hour allotted to a lesson would stretch out to an hour or more, if no other pupil was scheduled. Often, with Mrs. L. and Mrs. K., my last two teachers, none would be. It was clear to everyone, themselves included, that they were dedicated less to teaching than to the small sums their teaching brought in. This obvious fact did not embarrass them. Times were hard and we understood. Afternoons with them I remember now as always hot and summerlike, time going by at a slow pace, drawn out endlessly toward dusk like a long ritardando. Even in the winter months the electric fan might be set on the floor beside us, where it turned sometimes with a click like a metronome's. Yellow Schirmer editions of Czerny and Chopin lay stacked on the closed lid of a baby grand, along with assorted sheet music, popular and classical. Fan turning, teacher close beside me, I would run through the scales, the exercises, again and again.

My first piano teacher, a Mrs. Snow, was more inspiring. Only last week, looking through one of my mother's albums, I came across a snapshot of Mrs. Snow. Under a corner of sky now brown and faded she stands with smiling pupil, unidentified, in front of a cottage above whose entrance a signboard spells out MUSICLAND. She wears a choker of beads and clutches a crushed handkerchief. I had forgotten her double chin. The snapshot is not in color—too ancient for that—but the color of the flowered chiffon dress she is wearing in the picture does all the same come back to me, a bleached out coppery or rust tone. And now suddenly her very body odor, to which I must have grown accustomed as a child, comes back as well, secret and powdery. Sometimes there are these delicate small intimacies between teacher and pupil, never spoken of.

There was perhaps a touch of destiny in how we were brought together. One Saturday night my mother and father and I were downtown shopping, as we often were, for the stores stayed open well into the evening then. Heading back to our parked car along busy Miami Avenue, mother and I made a last sweep through the Cromer-Cassell's department store. There in the basement we came upon one of the rhythm bands which were a feature of that era, like Tom Thumb weddings and streetcorner evangelists. This band was just finishing up a per-formance; it must have been near closing time. Ten or twelve small children, all wearing overseas caps and blue-and-white shoulder-length capes, stood huddled together as they tapped and banged away at snare drums and wood blocks and triangles or shook their tambourines and castanets and tiny handbells, which were held up at ear level and jiggled. We paused, mother and I, to listen. They stood in two rows on a low platform struggling with the beat, following a sort of wand waved by the large fairy godmother of a woman who led them. This proved to be Mrs. Snow. I think my mother took my hand, seeing my enthrallment. I was not quite six years old, and I had not before then seen a musical group of any kind up close.

My wish was obvious, and before long I had a snare drum and cape of my own. (The drum was my sixth-birthday present; the receipt for it is pasted in a scrapbook—Cromer-Cassell's, $6.50.) Very soon the drum gave way to lessons on the piano. And none too soon for me. The sounds of the piano, in all their sonorities and relations, were a sort of heaven to me compared to the pitchless, snarly note of the snare.

Mrs. Snow was not only leader of the band but also gave piano lessons. The rhythm band was a sideline, mostly for show; at heart she was a serious musician. She had recently come south from Massachusetts. Her northern name evokes even now for me the whiteness of her hair and something also in her character that over the years was to remain remote and otherworldly, but she could be soft and melting too, motherly and enfolding to a child my age. How well the name suited her she realized, often commenting on it, with a little laugh. Snow itself was of course unknown to us in Miami, and even New Englanders were rare. Many people from the North had moved down to what we called the tropics for reasons of health, or so we assumed. Probably that was the case with Mrs. Snow herself, for she never looked truly well, now that I think of it. I remember still the thick white hose she had sometimes to wear over her swollen and empurpled legs. She saw no doctors, being a Christian Scientist. To stand with swollen legs must have been painful, but to stand for long periods conducting a dozen children with noisemakers would have been torment. Stoic though she was, she allowed herself a high stool then, upon which she could lean or sit back, with not much loss of dignity, keeping time with her baton.

Mrs. Snow believed in method and exactness, even for a pupil just starting school, like me. Along with her older pupils, I was required to take down during the first part of each lesson a simple sort of musical dictation. Upon our music pads, which bore the Baconian motto, "Writing makes the exact man," we would set down key signatures, notes, rests, scales, and, under guidance, a few harmonic progressions, chiefly cadences. Before long we were being encouraged to compose our own simple melodies, to be harmonized in consultation. Each week to our looseleaf notebooks was added a page containing the picture of a famous composer, which resembled in style the small busts commanding the mantelpiece and shelves and even some of the sills of the Snow cottage. For Christmas that year—it was 1931—I received from my teacher a T. Presser card, sentimentally tinted: the face of the young Mozart superimposed upon a photograph of his "Geburtshaus." How foreign it all seemed to me! Somewhere beyond Miami and the South of my family lay faraway New England and, beyond that, Europe, and in Europe were Germany and Austria, which I could picture as on a map with the birthplaces of the great composers indicated by dots. There may actually have been such a musical map for our notebooks.

Every Wednesday afternoon—I think it was Wednesday—my mother would pick me up after school in the old Essex she had only recently learned to drive. The first thing I would do then was open the lunch pail into which she would have packed a sandwich and cookies for the expedition, though it was a drive of not more than four or five miles. All day in the first-grade classroom I would have been aware of what day it was and of what the afternoon promised. By the time we were crossing the

17th Avenue bridge over the Miami River the sense of adventure would be strong in me. (This was not far from where the Orange Bowl now stands, and at that time it was an especially picturesque residential area, with quantities of red and yellow crotons along the approaches to the bridge, and a scattering of traveler's palms, not to mention the two or three small caves hidden in the rocks below.) It used to seem to me that we were crossing a sort of frontier into a different world, a fairytale world I would always be eager to enter.

My mother and I were soon members of a circle which may well have included every child in the city taking music lessons and, of course, their mothers. I wonder now what the grand building could have been in which musical galas and banquets of those years took place; I wonder where it could possibly have stood. It may have been Miami High School, from which I would graduate a decade or so later, but if so, the thought never crossed my mind while I was attending classes there. In any case, there was then somewhere a great labyrinthine building, of unusual intricacy, just the sort of building which makes an ideal setting for dreams, with numerous arches and arcades and courtyards. I remember one performance in a courtyard in which I took part. It was a pantomime enacting the story of Jonah and the Whale, one of several numbers during the course of a musical evening. I was small enough for Jonah, and a young man much larger than I played the Whale; I was to struggle free from our joint costume during the performance. I don't think I have actually dreamed about this since, but the memory does carry with it something of the phantasmagoric character of dreams. What it had to do with music escapes me now.

The little I knew of social and class distinctions I must have learned from those affairs. The near poor, like us, mingled quite democratically with the wealthy few. The glamor of it for me came more from the newness and strangeness than from any hints of wealth or fame. One or two retired coloraturas, whose names grew familiar through repeated appearances as sponsors on a succession of printed programs, represented the sum total of the local famous, musically. In 1932, when Paderewski appeared in concert, it was at the enormous Methodist church downtown known as the White Temple; from one of its balconies my mother and I, like hundreds of others, gazed down at a small man foreshortened by distance. Now and then, invited to a recital, we did glimpse the sumptuous interior of some splendid house. And there were occasional holiday parties, usually out-doors, behind massive vinecovered mortared walls, under tall palms. We children were often got up in costume for these, like juveniles attached to a touring stage company. All these years I have kept an impression of sparkling perfect teeth flashed by the seven- and eight-year-old beauties of those houses. Once, on a raised outdoor terrace, upon a glass-topped table the like of which I had never before seen, appeared a plate of tiny blue sand-wiches, cut into triangles. I wondered at once how *blue* would taste. No one seemed to be looking. I closed my fist over one or two of the tiny sandwiches, protectively, as over a catch of fire-flies, and made my way quickly down into the yard and around a corner to sample them in secret. They were delicious.

Our parents must have known—how could they have failed to know?—that nothing at all practical could come from any of this. The half-dollar each week was like a coin paid the gypsy for her improbable prophesyings or dropped into the collection plate at Sunday morning services, with a silent prayer. The giving and taking of such lessons goes on even now, I know, and probably for the same reasons as ever, but during the depression there may have been a special desperation in it all. The lessons may have represented a way out, the moral equivalent of boxing for the successive waves of immigrants—Irish, Jewish, Italian—who had hung around gyms with the hope of becoming champions. More than one of the little girls I knew, their mothers fallen un-der the spell of Shirley Temple, had their hair done in curls and studied tap dancing. Tap was the ballet of the poor, and at the end of a school day you could hear a confusion of shoetaps clat-tering off down the corridors of Allapattah Elementary. As for me, my Georgia aunts and uncles, during our summer round of visits, never failed to ask what I wanted to be when I grew up. Usually I had an answer ready—accountant, aviator, first-base-man—but such answers were polite fictions. It would not be for a long while yet that I would want to be anything in particular. Music was what I liked more than anything else, but I never envisioned myself in the long tails and with the streaming hair of a Paderewski, taking bows. All the same, I see now that, with my first lesson, just as my parents may have wished, I had begun to escape the lives we knew then—their life.

Even so, after two or three years, my lessons with Mrs. Snow came to an end. No more "March Militaire" at the Snow recitals for me, no more afterschool drives, no more blue sandwiches. It may be that Mrs. Snow had become too old and frail to meet the demands she put on herself. Perhaps she died or went back to New England. I wish I knew now; I think very kindly of her. She taught me the language of music, how to read and write it, and her training left me very quick at sightreading, a knack that has enabled me throughout my life to read through much of the literature for the piano, not without mistakes, but without hard work either, and with the pure, conscienceless pleasure of the amateur.

Or possibly, for a year or two, my parents simply could not afford the cost of lessons. But the family version, probably accurate, is that breaking off the lessons was my idea. There were days I am sure when, instead of practicing, I would rather have been out-of-doors with the other boys, playing ball. Music was coming to seem a soft and feminine world to me by then, and the practice hour was *very* solitary. I remember moments of impatience, the faint squeaking of the piano stool as it twisted in restless quarterturns beneath me, and all the while the voices of friends at play in the vacant lot directly across from our house. But now when I try to think back to that time I wonder if stopping the lessons may not have had something to do with the death just about then of my best friend, a bright and cheerful boy from down the street, as skinny and full of nerves as I was, who lingered on for months before his rheumatic fever finally killed him. His death terrified us that late spring when I was nine, all of us about his age who, dressed at our neatest, acted as pallbearers one sad afternoon. I was to weep off and on all summer, grievously. At some point during that period, I know, I was no longer taking piano lessons; that is all I can say for sure now. Before the summer was out I had fallen ill myself, with osteomyelitis, and during the long recuperation, which lasted through the winter and most of the next spring, there was no question of resuming lessons.

Our piano—the same upright, I believe, on which my mother had practiced her own lessons—never stayed in tune for long. I wish I could remember the name of its maker, but all I know is that it was not a Steinway, not a Baldwin, not a Chickering. It had a loud, bright, rather brassy sound which I had prized from the start. On it, pianissimo was far more difficult to manage than fortissimo, but in any case I preferred fortissimo. Once I stopped taking lessons the piano tuner no longer had to come around, a saving, but the seasons of neglect took their toll. This precious instrument, with its darkening and chipped ivories, two or three of them glued back on slightly askew, went on sliding slowly downward out of tune, always downward, flatter and flatter, but unevenly flat from note to note. Some of the resulting combinations, different from month to month, used to fascinate me. I could strike some favorite dissonance repeatedly, thrilled by its oddness. How far its pitch had sunk overall came home to me when friends from the school band had to make dramatic adjustments to their horns to bring them into tune with our upright's B♭. Finally, it seemed to have settled into being almost exactly half a tone flat, resisting all efforts to make it hold a truer pitch, like an elderly person no longer willing to dress up for the world at large. I can still remember the unique plangency of its B just below middle C (actually B♭). The resonance of that note remains in my ear as a prototype of all future resonances.

It was my friend Coney who encouraged me to ask for lessons again. He loved music, loved picking out tunes and harmonies at our odd-sounding piano, and had somehow taught himself to read music, probably with a clue or two from me. About my age, twelve or so, he needed lessons of his own, from a real teacher, but was shy about getting started and wanted company. We began lessons about the same time from Mrs. L., a neighbor, who wore long, colorful skirts and seemed almost to belong to the same generation as her own daughter. Thought to be separated from her husband, she augmented her doubtful income by offering lessons in dance as well, both ballroom and tap. Her daughter danced with fire and spirit and could play the piano with a certain brave flair, a living advertisement for her mother's skills. Coney lived a couple of blocks farther than I did from our teacher's house, and along the way had to pass a small grocery. On lesson afternoons he would sometimes be seen hurrying down 19th Avenue, late as usual, a paper sack bulging with soft-drink bottles clutched to his chest. These Coney would turn in at the grocery for the two-cents deposit on each. The family who ran the grocery may have hated to see him coming, but the proceeds enabled him to pay for the week's lesson with Mrs. L.

I like to think now that our experience was not unusual. Among the hundred thousand or so people in the Miami of the thirties there would have been six or seven other teachers like Mrs. L., if not more. And, in the nation at large, who can guess how many? There must often have been a man in the background, whose chief stay and support the teacher was. During one of those moments in lessons when the eye begins to wander, the pupil might catch a glimpse of this mysterious figure, as I did once, though not at Mrs. L.'s. Outdoors he sat, ensconced in a sort of deck chair, under the shade of fruit trees, staring out across an ocean of halfmown grass at nothing, nothing at all. Did they drink, these lost men? Were they the victims of shell shock, or tuberculosis? Mrs. L.'s husband was none of these, but wrapped in a deeper mystery still. We saw little of him, for he was Hispanic and lived, as we pieced the story together, in Cuba. His visits were always brief, always unexpected. Suddenly he would be stepping off the bus that stopped at our corner. He was a small, fragile-looking person who carried himself stiffly and dressed in a black that seemed unnatural in that climate. The effort to recall this ghostly personage turns up a cane for him as well. Past one interested porch after another he would proceed, touching the tip of his cane gingerly to the sidewalk before him, like someone experimenting with the idea of blindness. A diplomat of sorts, or so we had been allowed to gather. Where the idea had come from that he showed up only to demand money from Mrs. L. I am not sure. Perhaps at some point she complained of this weakness to my mother. In any case, we always suspected the worst of him, this courtly-looking little man who came and went like something in a dream.

Before long Coney and I found ourselves beyond Mrs. L's scope as a teacher. She must have known this time would come, and she remained sympathetic, interested in our futures. Mrs. K. followed as my teacher. I used to ride my bicycle to her house, a mile or so distant. The greater distance I had to cover seemed for a while like a measure of progress. I would pedal through the sultry afternoons, working up to a furious speed and then coasting, no hands, music books safe in the wire basket clipped to the handlebars. Mrs. K. herself could take me only so far into the piano literature—somewhere among the black keys of Chopin—but this proved to be just about as far as I really wanted to go at the time. The moods of the nocturnes and the ballades, dreamy and bittersweet, as they seemed then to me, were exactly right for someone just beginning to drift through the lovely-dark passages of adolescence. Sometimes I would move over on the piano bench while Mrs. K. demonstrated how to handle a certain passage. And the few bars might extend themselves all the way to the end of the piece, for at such times Mrs. K. was capable of forgetting herself. Transported, she would become another person. As the passionate notes of one or the other of the nineteenth-century Romantics, her specialty, sprang to life beneath her suddenly invigorated fingers, she seemed to rise briefly into some sphere of romance herself. Her tensed hands would rebound upwards from the keys then, to quiver suspended above the final echoing chord, while she turned her head toward me and smiled, as if we shared a secret. Even as I returned the smile, she would be subsiding back into her ordinary self. This was not an illusion of mine. Clearly she felt something of it too, and this must have cast over her life a thin shadow of regret, the sort of mild discontent which adds a touch of mysterious interest to the characters of otherwise unexceptional persons. In the case of Mrs. K., the effect was purely transitory. Only when she was, so to speak, inspired by the miraculously rapid and precise movements of her own fingers, as if she herself might not quite understand what was happening, did this second Mrs. K. bob to the surface, and then only for a few seconds at a time.

There seemed to be no one in Miami who could teach me what I really wanted to learn, which was to compose music. Already, without knowing nearly enough, I was composing what I could, obsessively. So was my friend Coney. We bought score-paper at Amidon's Music Store downtown and filled it with thousands of notes, a form of magic. At fifteen I wrote a long piece grandly entitled "Myth" and intended for an orchestra larger than any I had yet heard. But when finally, after weeks of hesitation, I inquired of Mrs. K. whom I could study composition with, she had no idea. She lent me her harmony textbook from the conservatory. That was all very well, but limited, and I was by then looking for something vaster, more challenging. Sometimes I felt that no one had confidence in me but myself. There was my mother, but she would have believed in me without any reason. A few years later—and, as I sometimes feel, too late, after the critical moment had passed—I was to meet the composer Carl Ruggles, Ives' friend, who wintered in Miami, and he very willingly took me on as a free pupil. Then, amply, the confidence which can be so important to the young was given me, and in it I beamed and I basked, proud, happy, looking to the future. Had I met Ruggles at thirteen or fourteen I wonder if I might not now be writing music, very contentedly, whether in Hollywood (as I secretly imagine) or in some academy or conservatory.

For several years I felt not so much lost as suspended in a sort of vacuum. I had the sense of trying to make headway against some unseen obstacle, as in anxiety dreams. Meanwhile I read the books available in the public library. Teaching myself to read orchestral scores, I read through what there was of Haydn, Mozart, Beethoven—nothing in the library then so new as Debussy. It may be hard for anyone now to grasp how difficult recordings were to come by, and especially of new music. I remember listening for the first time—and with what shocked delight—to Stravinsky's *Firebird*, an orchestral commonplace now, and perhaps even then already so. But how could I have known? And at the sudden explosion of the whole orchestra at the start of the king's "infernal dance," I am sure that my face must have flushed with excitement, there in the isolation of the listening booth. With a curious logic, this booth happened to be located on the mezzanine of the same department store where mother and I had first encountered Mrs. Snow's rhythm band. (The name of the store had been changed to Richards' by then.) There too I first heard the other Stravinsky ballets and an early recording of Schoenberg's *Pierrot Lunaire*, featuring Erika Mann, Auden's proxy bride. The recording could not have been made long after she arrived in this country, fleeing Europe. Only the summer before I had read her father's *The Magic Mountain*. Things seemed to fit together somehow.

I used to wonder who in all of Miami could finally have purchased the single copy of the Schoenberg album, which had stood for weeks unclaimed on the shelf. I could not afford to buy it myself, but I returned to it. Then one week it was gone. I never really believed that it had been shipped to Miami for me alone, but I did think that no one else in the city—in the whole state of Florida, for that matter—could have appreciated it just then the way I did. (I still believe that.) I could almost have thought the recording had been made for just that moment of revelation when I had first touched needle to groove in the listening booth at Richards' and heard the high, harsh *Sprechstimme* ringing forth. Such are the grandiosities of adolescence.

1 IT WAS A KIND AND NORTHERN FACE: MRS. SNOW

Busts of the great composers
Glimmered in niches, pale stars—
                    and Mrs. Snow
Could tower above her pupils like an alp,
An avalanche threatening sudden
Unasked for kindnesses.
                    Exiled, alone,
She did not quite complain,
But only sighed and looked off elsewhere,
Regretting the Symphony perhaps.
                    In dreams, though,
The new palms of the yard,
The one brilliant flame tree
Must have changed back into the elms and maples
Of old, decaying streets.
—Sometimes the inadequate floor quaked
With the effort of her rising.
The great legs, swollen and empurpled,
Could hardly support the hugeness
Of her need.
                    And if
They did not understand—her friends—
She had, in any case, the artistic
Temperament,
                    which isolates—
And saves!
                    Dust motes
Among the Chinese jars. Etchings
Of Greece and Rome. The photograph
Of Mrs. Eddy.
                    Brown sky, so old,
Fading above us all.

2 BUSTED DREAMS: MRS. K.

The faint odour of your patchouli . . .

The mother's gypsy skirt
Flared like the daughter's.
                 Together
They demonstrated the foxtrot,
Gliding across the living room
And back, each time avoiding
With the same heartbreaking little swoop
                       or dip
The shabby, cloth-draped, pushed-back, suddenly looming
Sofa.
               On the piano top,
A nest of souvenirs:
               paper
Flowers, old programs, a broken fan,
Like a bird's broken wing.
—And sometimes Mr. L. himself
Returned, compulsive, like a dream.
                 He would have brought
Real flowers. Thin,
Demanding, his voice soared after dark
In the old opera between them.
But no one saw the blows, only
An occasional powdered bruise,
Genteel. Did he come all the way from
Cuba each time for this?
                The children
Were loosed upon the neighborhood
To wander. In the summer-idle
Schoolyard they were the last ghosts
Of the swings.
          Nine o'clock, ten o'clock.
A thousand reconcilings.
             The moon . . .
                Next day,
On the Havana ferryboat again,
A little, overneat man at the rail,
Examining the waves, his nails.

And she,
Plunging the stiff comb suddenly deep
Into her hair, would be just turning
To greet some half-forgotten pupil at the door.

3 THOSE TROPIC AFTERNOONS: MRS. K.

But in Miami?

Four or five o'clock.
                    Late summer
Around us like a cocoon,
Gauzy and intimate.
—And sometimes she succumbed
To the passion of a nocturne,
The fury of the climax
Ascending through the folds
Of secret and abandoned flesh
Into those bitten finger-ends
That pressed from the unsuspecting keys
A certain exaltation—
Only to die away at last
Into the long fermata.

(Satisfaction. The brief
And inward smile.)
                  Meanwhile,
Dappled with shade of tangelo and mango,
In canvas deck chair that sagged,
                  the husband
Sat peering out across
A forlorn sea of halfmown lawn,
Balding, out of work, a sad
Columbus.
                Some drone
Of traffic, far off, seemed
To reassure: 54th Street still
Led off toward the Glades at sunset.

And I—
What had I to be afraid of?—
The yellow lesson book
Open on the rack
To that blue, lofty look of hers
That used to float there, cloudlike.
                    The fan,
Placed on the floor, clicked
With every turn—metronome
Of boredom.
                    Once more, dear: Larghetto.
Infinities receding.
                    Laborers
Coming home, the long day ending.

The Pupil

Picture me, the shy pupil at the door,
One small, tight fist clutching the dread Czerny.
Back then time was still harmony, not money,
And I could spend a whole week practicing for
That moment on the threshold.
                              Then to take courage,
And enter, and pass among mysterious scents,
And sit quite straight, and with a frail confidence
Assault the keyboard with a childish flourish!

Only to lose one's place, or forget the key,
And almost doubt the very metronome
(Outside, the traffic, the laborers going home),
And still to bear on across Chopin or Brahms,
Stupid and wild with love equally for the storms
Of C# minor and the calms of C.

Afterschool Practice: An Episode

Rain that masks the world
Presses it back too hard against
His forehead at the pane.
Three stories down, umbrellas
Are borne along the current of the sidewalk; a bus
Glides like a giant planchette
In some mysterious pattern through the traffic.
Alone now, he feels lost in the new apartment;
He feels some dark cloud shouldering in.
His wish, if he could have one,
Would be for the baby next door to cry out
This minute, signifying end of nap.
Then he could practice. (Apartment life
Is full of these considerations.)
But when finally this does happen,
He still for a time postpones the first chord.
He looks around, full of secrets;
His strange deep thoughts have brought, so far, no harm.
Carefully, with fists and elbows, he prepares
One dark, tremendous chord
Never heard before—his own thunder!
And strikes.
            And the strings will quiver with it
A long time before the held petal
Gives up the sound completely—this throbbing
Of the piano's great exposed heart.
Then, soberly, he begins his scales.

And gradually the storm outside dies away also.

The Sunset Maker

The speaker is a friend of the dead com-
poser, Eugene Bestor. He is seated on the
terrace of his condominium, from which
there is a view of the Gulf of Mexico.

The Bestor papers have come down to me.
I would imagine, though, they're destined for
The quiet archival twilight of some library.
Meanwhile, I have been sorting through the scores.
I linger sometimes over his last piece,
The 'Elegy.' I seem to see the notes
Flying above the staff like flags of mourning;
And I can hear the sounds the notes intend.
(Some duo of the mind produces them,
Without error, ghostmusic materializing;
Faintly, of course, like whispers overheard.)
And then? I might work up the piano part,
If it mattered. But where is there a cellist
This side of the causeway? And who plays Bestor now?

This time of day I listen to the surf
Myself; I listen to it from my terrace.
The sun eases its way down through the palms,
Scattering colors—a bit of orange, some blues.
Do you know that painting of Bonnard's, *The Terrace*?
It shows a water pitcher blossom-ready
And a woman who bends down to the doomed blossoms—
One of the fates, in orange—and then the sea
With its own streaks of orange, harmonious.
It used to hang in the Phillips near the Steinway.
But who could call back now the web of sound
The cello and the piano spun together
In the same Phillips not so long ago?
The three plucked final chords—someone might still
Recall, if not the chords, then the effect
They made—as if the air were troubled somehow.
As if . . . but everything there is is that.
The cello had one phrase, an early phrase,
That does stay with me. (It may be mixed by now

With Bonnard's colors.) A brief rush upward, then
A brief subsiding. Can it be abstract?—
As Stravinsky said it must be to be music.
But what if a phrase *could* represent a thought—
Or feeling, should we say?—without existence
Apart from the score where someone catches it?

Inhale, exhale: a drawn out gasp or sigh.
Falling asleep, I hear it. It is just there.
I don't say what it means. And I agree
It's sentimental to suppose my friend
Survives in just this fragment, this tone-row
A hundred people halfway heard one Sunday
And one of them no more than half remembers.
The hard early years of study, those still,
Sequestered mornings in the studio,
The perfect ear, the technique, the great gift
All have come down to this one ghostly phrase.
And soon nobody will recall the sound
These six notes made once or that there were six.

Hear the gulls. That's our local music.
I like it myself; and, as you can see,
Our sunset maker studied with Bonnard.

Little Elegy for Cello and Piano

It was early December, still warm. Damp leaves were packed thickly against the curbs that afternoon as we walked; others had stuck to the sidewalks or left their imprint there, a season's decalcomania.

Being early, we had time for a sort of tea at an outdoor cafe. It was just warm enough to sit outdoors under the canopy without discomfort, probably the last Sunday of the year when that would still be so. Looking back now, I see that there must have been something of the poignancy of last occasions in the air, even though we were not much aware of it at the time. I remember the barely legible script of the oversized menus and the cheerful waitresses darting and hovering about in their starchy sky-blue smocks. From time to time laughter arose from the tables around us.

There was a moment when Eugene folded his hand over my sister Florence's hand on the checkered tablecloth and smiled. When Eugene smiled broadly like that it always seemed to me that his domed bald head took on a slight glow as from some inner illumination. He and my sister had been married for more than thirty years, and it was clear that they had weathered out whatever storms had come their way. The waitress, bringing our hot cocoa and small pastries, took in the situation at a glance and beamed with an air of almost parental approval.

What we found to talk about I have forgotten. Someone unseen walked past on the sidewalk, whistling a jagged little up-to-date tune none of us could identify. It amused us, not knowing. There was the aroma of Eugene's after-tea cigar suspended among us, blending with the smell of dregs and cake crumbs, of scrubbed bodies and clean clothes. And the December sunshine continued to pour down. Overhead, beyond the canopy, the sky was cloudless.

We may have lingered, or perhaps the cheerful service was slow. We had to hurry, after all, through streets strangely empty. We passed a few of the lesser embassies, where little knots of people—journalists, we supposed—stood about waiting for someone to arrive or to depart. Perhaps it was a day on which something important was expected, but if so I have forgotten what it was. At one of the embassies—I don't know Washington very well—a limousine did turn up the semicircular drive just as we reached the corner, and we stood for a moment watching while several dark-costumed mysterious bodies were disgorged and swept indoors before any harm could be done to them. It was one of those small but definite events, of no significance or consequence, which nevertheless seem instantly memorable.

By the time we had gone up the steps to the Phillips Collection, the foyer seemed crowded. Small groups were just beginning to drift towards the gallery where the chairs were set out for the afternoon's recital. Florence disappeared almost at once into the back room where her cello waited. Although one of his pieces was on the program that afternoon, Eugene was not widely enough known as a composer to be much recognized. All the same, as we edged past the music stand and the open grand, two or three glances were cast in his direction. Eugene was oblivious to that, as usual. The Steinway gleamed. Eugene paused beside the open piano, I noticed, looking down as if to ponder his own reflection in the polished black.

We found seats, among the last untaken. They were in the corner next to the immense Bonnard, "La Grande Terrasse." The painted couple in the bright foreground struck me at once as a couple much like Florence and Eugene, now translated improbably into a sort of paradise made up all of flowers and light. One reason I had never passed much beyond the amateur stage myself as a musician was a tendency on my part to drift off, while listening, on some fantasy or other, as if the music were nothing more than an accompaniment to my all too cinematic visions. Except when actually playing, I could never attend to music as music for very long at a time, though I had always loved it. And that afternoon, in spite of my good intentions, I knew that the world of Bonnard would be an added temptation to drift.

I duly noted Florence, changed now into long dark skirt, as she entered and executed her neat bow, along with the pianist, a tiny man with several large rings on his fingers, also bowing neatly and smiling. Beyond, at the other end of the room, the weakening sunlight filtered in through the narrow screens onto the bronze peacock and the slender reaching limbs of a potted plant on a table. But with the first notes of the Fauré with which the performance was launched I was already wandering off down the painted terrace at my shoulder toward the sea and a sky flocked with gold and lavender clouds.

The first thing I really registered was the half-moment of

silence when the Fauré was done. I applauded with the rest. And now I noticed a singular stillness descending on Eugene. His "Little Elegy for Cello and Piano" was next on the program. I saw how perfectly one could be tuned to listen. Eugene had become a listener. He was like some instrument made for that purpose—like a raingauge, to catch rainwater. I could see his shoulders hunching, his breath drawing in. It is one of the ways I like to picture him. Then the piano began its little storm and almost as suddenly grew still. Florence's bow drew out a long note in the middle range and held it; and then, as she and the bejeweled pianist began their mournful dialogue, I saw Eugene's very jowls slacken with pleasure and contentment.

The piece was a sort of fantasia in one long movement. By *long* I mean ten or twelve minutes at most. But I had in fact lost track of time. There was a perfect consonance between the Bonnard and Eugene's music. I thought I could read also on the faces of those nearest me a sheen of attention that went beyond politeness or curiosity. And I sensed or imagined in Eugene himself a fulfillment which must come very rarely. Florence was bent close to her instrument, drawing from it the rich, exact sounds the composer had conceived, but now they took on an existence apart from him. They had momentarily a life in and of themselves, beyond us all.

At some point during the performance Eugene sneezed. There had been the usual muffled coughs and rustlings and shiftings all along, but the ear adjusts to familiar disruptions without difficulty. This sneeze of his was somehow different. It succeeded in obliterating one rapid little staircase of notes. It was like a small rip in a garment, and I felt the loss even then, sharply and immediately.

The last sounds rescued me from the terrace—a succession of three plucked chords on the cello, quickly fading. Florence's familiar head with its bands of graypiled hair remained bowed briefly over her cello, and she did not look up in our direction. Probably Eugene had asked her not to. For when heads began to swivel around in search of the composer, and a few swung our way, Eugene remained seated. He preferred his anonymity.

During intermission a number of his and Florence's musical friends from the area came over and there was much pumping of hands. "Wonderful piece!" one friend exclaimed, and others joined in the praise.

I myself have always considered the "Little Elegy for Cello and Piano" Eugene Bestor's masterpiece. Ten or twelve minutes of music, no more, but hardly to be improved upon—sad, regretful, complete.

And yet it has not been heard since. Eugene died late that spring. Other works of the Bestor canon occasionally are heard, compositions longer established, but after the death of an artist one of two things generally happens. Either there is a rebirth of interest in his work, or else all interest wanes and withers quickly. The latter is by far the more common case, and so it has been with Eugene's music, however much respected it once was.

There was a memorial recital, but Florence was not in the mood to attempt the "Little Elegy" again so soon. She may have considered the piece too close in spirit to the occasion. She wanted bright pieces only, and it was her choice. Then, too, she may have wondered a little, as I did at the time, whether Eugene had had some early hint or premonition of his death to come, whether he might not have written the piece, in a sense, for himself. This, understandably, she would not have wanted to cope with for a while.

Two or three years later I learned from a program Florence mailed me that the "Little Elegy" was to be done at a college in Vermont near which the Bestors had lived. She knew my high opinion of the work. It was included on her initiative, I am sure, for she was the featured performer of the evening. But as luck would have it, she fell ill a day or two before the performance and the program had to be canceled at the last minute. Apparently it was a hard-luck piece, a jinx perhaps, as certain plays are said to be. Florence herself, I know, never again played it in public, and now she is gone also.

The Bestor manuscripts have come down to me. One day, I suppose, the library of the college in Vermont will have them. I used to take out the manuscript of Eugene's final composition now and then and let my eye run over the spidery calligraphy of the notes. The small black notes climbed the staves slowly or floated above the top line like miniature storm clouds. There was a visual drama to all this, and I had enough training to hear faintly the skeletal sounds behind the notes. But the music was a little beyond my practical skills. I could pick out the notes of the piano part at my own pace and work up the difficult passages, but it was not the same as performing it. In any case, there was not a cellist—none I had heard of anyhow—in the entire sprawling range and extent of the sun-and-sand community I had retired to recently. Perhaps there would have been one in the nearest junior college, but that was miles and miles away, back across the causeway.

There comes a time of day now when I sit back and listen to the surf. It is too far away to be seen but I can hear it. The sun is just easing its way down, scattering color. There is a terrace of my own out there, bricks, with potted palm tree and potted orange tree. I can hear the music better where I sit than at the keyboard. And I wonder how many others who were present in the Phillips that afternoon—an occasion neither heroic nor historic—can still summon up any of the by now broken web of sounds produced then, as I am able to do, though of course only partially and just barely. The last three plucked chords—surely the sound of them hangs on, consciously or not, in the memory of a few others, though fading.

There is one phrase of the cello's—an early phrase, before the sounds had become mixed up in my mind with Bonnard's colors—which holds fast for me, a little upward rush and subsiding of notes that has come to represent some nameless feeling which otherwise has no voice or expression. This is the way it is written out in the manuscript:

A brief inhaling and exhaling, a somewhat drawn out deep gasp or sigh. Sometimes this phrase comes to me just as I am falling asleep. It is not exactly that I hear it. It is just there, and I do not of course know what it means.

It is sentimental of me to think of Eugene as surviving through this fragment, which in any case I am probably the only person anywhere to remember. And yet it does seem as if all the hard early years of study and practice here and abroad, the thousands of mornings of seclusion in his studio, the remarkable ear, the near-photographic memory and recall, had all come down to this, this one ghostly phrase. And soon there will be no one at all to remember how even these six notes sounded.

The Artificial Moonlight

Coconut Grove, 1958

The Langs, Hal and his wife Julie, were giving a party.

From the screen porch of their apartment you could see, strung out across the bay, the colored lights of the neighborhood sailing club—the Langs did not belong—and, farther out, the bulky shadows of the members' boats riding at anchor. Almost always, with nightfall, there would be a breeze. It came from the bay and across the bayshore road past the shaggy royal palms bordering the driveway, cooling the porch like a large and efficient fan.

But tonight was one of those rare end-of-summer nights without any saving breeze. It was past midnight, and still the apartment felt oppressive and close. The heat was spoiling the party. It was a going-away party for an old friend of the Langs', Jack Felton, whom they saw now only when he came home from graduate school to visit his parents, and in a day or two, with summer over, he would be taking off for Europe on a Fulbright. But it was not only the heat. Some vague melancholy of departure and change seemed to have settled over everyone and everything.

In the back room a record player was turning, unattended. Sounds of the jazz of a dozen years ago, early Sarah Vaughan, drifted out to the porch. The casual guests, the friends of friends, had all departed. The few who remained looked settled in, as though they might stay forever, listless and bored, some on the sagging wicker chair and settee, and some on the floor cushions brought out from the stuffy back rooms. They looked as though they might never move again, not even to flip the stack of records when the music ended.

If anyone did, it would probably be Julie herself. Of the Langs, Julie was the dependable one. Five afternoons a week she worked as a legal stenographer, while her husband kept up appearances by giving occasional painting lessons to the daughters of tourists. Yet except for a shortage of money from time to time they lived with as much freedom from care and nearly as much leisure as the well-to-do. Approaching their thirties, they seemed as perpetually youthful as movie stars.

The odd hours they kept could be hard on Julie, and occasionally she retired early. She would be so wound up that she could not sleep and would have to read for a long time before her eyes closed. It was an intense sort of reading, beyond simple pleasure. One wall of their bedroom was filled with books, and sometimes when they made love without turning the lights off she caught herself innocently letting her eyes rove across the titles on the spines of the larger books. Once or twice Hal had complained of this publicly, to her embarrassment, but she seemed unable to change.

Alone in their bedroom, reading or not, she liked the sound of conversation floating back late at night from the porch. It was soothing, like the quiet, washing sound of an ocean. It was hot back here, and there was a little fan she could reach out for and turn on, but she did not often use it. She liked the warm weather; she could not imagine living anywhere but Miami.

Still, there were nights when Julie felt left out of things. Their friends all drank, and, except on the most ceremonial occasions, Julie did not. Of course the feeling went beyond that. She would suspect them of planning something incalculably exciting from which she was to be excluded. Unreasonable, but there was nothing she could do about the feeling. Julie gazed with half-closed eyes across the porch at her husband, where he sat perched on an arm of the old wicker settee, bending down to speak to a tall blond woman in slacks. She wondered if she would ever be able to trace this feeling of hers back to its source. How far back would she have to go? She was an orphan, adopted by a couple old enough to be her grandparents, long ago dead. Could it be as simple as that? She thought, sometimes, that she might have Spanish blood. That would account for her dark coloring, for her thick black eyebrows, her almost blue-black hair, which only a few days before she had cut short, despite Hal's protests.

In the back room now the record stopped and another dropped down from the stack—Duke Ellington, slow and bluesy. Shutting her eyes, Julie took a sip of the plain orange juice in her glass and, leaning back, crossed her legs. One tiny sandaled foot, the nails that afternoon painted a deep bloodred for the party, commenced to swing nervously back and forth, back and forth, to some inner rhythm of her own.

However serious his life elsewhere might have become, Jack had kept his old reputation locally for stirring things up. He wondered if the others were waiting for him to take some initiative now. After all, the party was for him.

But he was not the same person they remembered, not really. Whenever he came back home now it was as if the curtain had risen on a new act, with the same actors, but the playwright had without notice altered the course of the action. It was impossible to point to a time when everything had been as it should be, but that time must have existed once. They all felt it. And lately, to Jack, every change—the divorce of one couple, the moving away of another—came as an unwelcome change.

As for himself, Jack knew that he seemed quieter than he used to seem. In fact, he was. He had no wish to pretend otherwise, but in a very small way, just as he could imagine his friends doing, he missed his old self. He sat now very quietly, stretched out on his floor cushion, leaning back against the wall, his long legs folded in a lazy tangle before him. He looked half-asleep. But behind his glasses his eyes were still open. It might have seemed that he was listening to the music, except that it had stopped.

He had intended to listen. He had stacked the records himself, some of his favorites. Then, just as the unforgotten sounds had begun to bear him back toward his own adolescence, it had struck him suddenly why the girl sitting beside him, to whom he had been talking desultorily for the last twenty minutes or so, was wearing so loose and unbecoming a blouse—tardily, for she was, if not very far along, nevertheless visibly pregnant. To Jack, who had known her all his life, the realization came like a blow. When those very records were being cut, this girl, Susan, who was almost certainly the youngest person in the room, had been listening obediently to the nuns of her grammar school, wearing the blue-and-white uniform Jack still remembered. The summer before, when he had last seen her, Susan had not even been married. And already her husband, Robert or Bob, the sallow, sleepy-looking fellow in the corner who never had much to say, had got her pregnant.

For the time being Jack could concentrate on nothing but this, this fact that to him seemed so irremediably, if obscurely, wrong.

*   *   *

Hal was bending down, whispering into the blond woman's ear. Not that there was anything important to be said, but there was a pleasure in merely leaning toward her in that way, some momentary illusion of intimacy. What he had to say was only that soon they would be out of vodka.

And then he sighed. There was a sort of perfume coming, apparently, from a spot just behind her ear. Green was her married name, Karen Green, and Hal had known her longer than he had known his wife. As far back as high school he had had a hopeless crush on her, but never before had he noticed how peculiarly large and yet shapely her left ear was, from which the hair was drawn back, and how many little whorls it contained, impossible to count. Was she wearing her hair some new way?

Hal leaned closer and whispered, "Of course we could always go out to Fox's for more. More vodka."

It was half a question. It was the tone he always adopted with Karen, the tone of casual flirtation, just as though they were in school together still.

A rustling stirred in the palms outside, the first sign of something like a breeze. For a moment the wind rose, the rolled tarpaulins high up on the screen seemed to catch their breath.

All at once, borne to them on the faint edge of wind, they heard a dance band playing, not very far away, a rumba band —snarling trumpet, bongo drums, maracas. Had it been playing all this time? Everyone listened. Jack straightened up and peered about the room, somewhat crossly, like a person roused from an interesting dream.

"The Legion dance," someone called out.

The large, good-looking man, who from his cushion beside Julie Lang's chair had also been watching Hal and the blond woman, climbed to his feet. This was Sid Green, Karen's husband. Standing, he loomed larger than anyone else in the group.

Normally unassertive, Sid heard his own voice calling across the porch, "Hey, Hal, you by any chance a member?" To himself his voice sounded unexpectedly loud, as if it contained some challenge he did not wish to issue more directly.

"For Christ's sake, Sid, the *Foreign* Legion maybe, not the American."

"If somebody was a member, we could go to the dance," Sid said. "I mean if anybody wanted to."

"Crash it?" the pregnant girl asked.

"Oh, maybe not," Sid said, looking around, and even his flash of enthusiasm was fading.

"I don't know," Hal said, with a glance at Sid's wife beside him.

"Oh, let's do go!" Julie cried out suddenly from across the porch. "For God's sake, let's do something! Just wait a minute till I change my shoes." And kicking her sandals off, fluffing her short crop of hair out as she went, she hurried back through the dark apartment toward the bedroom.

But when she returned it was apparent that something was wrong. Hal and Karen were missing, and Jack as well. Julie peered into the corner where the other women were sitting—Susan and a girl named Annabelle, who appeared to be sound asleep.

"Aren't you coming?" Julie asked nervously.

"Not me," Susan said, placing one hand on her stomach. "Not in my condition." Her silent husband beamed, as if Susan had said something witty or perhaps flattering to him.

Julie felt more uncomfortable than ever. She had never been a mother, and she was a good deal older than Susan, seven or eight years at least, but she did not think that Susan and her husband would intentionally try to embarrass her. Everyone knew that she had never wanted children, that she preferred her freedom.

Julie turned to Sid; their eyes met. He was quiet, too quiet to be amusing in the way that Hal and even Jack could sometimes be, but really quite good-looking in his athletic fashion, dark and mysterious, withheld. They knew very little about Sid. Was it true that his family had money? If only, Julie thought, he would volunteer himself more, like Hal. But at least Sid could be managed.

"Come on, you," she said, taking him by the hand and pulling. "Let's catch up with the others."

Meekly, Sid allowed himself to be led out the door.

On the dock it was very quiet. Only stray phrases of the Cuban trumpet carried out that far.

As they had walked out onto the dock, which was floated on

an arrangement of great, slowly rusting oil drums, it had bobbed and swayed with every step. By now it had settled down. The three of them—Hal and Karen and Jack—sat dangling their legs over the end, looking out at the anchored boats rocking on the water. Above the water, very bright, as if left over from some festivity, were strung the lights of the sailing club. All of the lights together cast a strange glow on the dark waters of the bay, a thin swath of artificial moonlight which reached out perhaps halfway toward the long, indistinct blur of the nearest island.

Jack wanted to touch the water, see how cold it was. Carefully, he set the drink he had brought with him down upon the planking and removed his loafers.

Not that he meant to swim. But as he thrust one leg down, and his toes touched water, which was not as cold as expected, he found himself thinking of a woman they all knew, a woman named Roberta, who had once lived in the apartment above the Langs, and how she sometimes used to swim out to the island, which was no more than a dark, low line on the horizon. There was nothing to do out there; it was a mere piney arm of sand. She would wait just long enough to catch her breath and then swim back. That was all. It would not have been, if you were a swimmer, very dangerous. There were plenty of boats along the way to catch hold of if you tired.

Perhaps they were all thinking of Roberta just then, for when Hal asked, out of the blue, if they knew that Roberta was in San Francisco, Karen said, "Funny, I was just thinking of that time she drove her car into the bay."

"Well, not quite all the way in," Hal said. "It stalled, you know."

Hal was the authority on the stories they told about people they used to know. There was a good-sized collection of them, recounted so often the identities of the participants tended to blur, and the facts themselves were subject to endless small revisions and adjustments.

"I thought it was a palm tree that stopped her," Jack commented, rather sourly. He had never been one of Roberta's admirers. At the time, she had seemed a silly romantic girl, mad for attention. He tried to recall her face but could not. Had it been pretty? He seemed to remember it as pale, rather moon-shaped, but perhaps that was someone else's, someone more elusive still.

"You're right," Hal agreed. "There was a palm tree somewhere, but where?" He began to reconstruct. "The car must have caromed off the palm and gone on into the bay. Yes, partway in. I seem to picture it hanging over the edge, sort of."

"I always thought she did it on purpose," Karen said.

"No, it was an accident." On that point Hal was definite.

Gradually a deeper melancholy settled over them. All around, the small dinghies tied up at the dock nosed familiarly against the wood. One was painted a vivid orange and white, the colors of the sailing club. A car passed behind them along the bayshore road, swiftly, heading for Miami proper.

Karen looked out across the bay. "Well, she should have done it on purpose. That would have made sense. It would have been—oh, I don't know . . ."

Off and on all evening Jack had been wondering what, if anything, was on between Hal and Karen. Karen was very beautiful, more beautiful than she had been ten years ago, just out of high school, when everyone, himself and Hal too, as he remembered, was buzzing around her. Experience had only ripened her; she made him think of some night-blooming flower the neighbors call you out to see. Probably just then—at that very minute, Jack would have liked to believe—she was at the absolute peak of her beauty. The next summer, surely by the summer after, she would have crossed the invisible line they were all approaching. On the other side of that line strangers would no longer find her quite so remarkable to look at, only old friends like Hal and himself, who would remember her face as it had been lit momentarily by the driftwood fire of some otherwise forgotten beach picnic, or more likely as it was now, shaped by the glow of the lights strung out from the dock over the water.

He recalled a story of Hal's, a story he did not much like to think of, of how Hal and a girl Jack didn't know had rowed out to the island one night and stayed till dawn. Thinking about the story now, with the island itself so near, Jack began to feel curiously giddy, as if the dock were starting to bob again.

"What about the island?" he asked.

"What about it?" Karen said.

"What about going out to the island?"

"I couldn't swim that far," she said. "Not nearly."

"Not swim. We borrow one of these dinghy things. Ask Hal. He's done it before."

Hal grinned. "Right. The night watchman, he sleeps back in that little shack. Besides, he doesn't really give a damn."

In a moment they were climbing down into the orange-and-white dinghy, a trickier operation than it looked. Whenever one of them put a foot down, exploring, the boat seemed to totter almost to the point of capsizing. Jack could not hold back a snort of laughter.

"Shh," Hal said.

"I thought he didn't give a damn," Karen said, tittering.

"Shh," Jack said. "Shh."

Once they were all seated, Hal took up the oars. They were just casting off, Jack had just managed to slip the rope free, when they heard footsteps coming up the walk. The rope dropped with a thick splash.

"Hey, we see you down there," a voice called, and Karen recognized it as her husband's. Just behind him stood Julie, their shadows bent out over the water.

"Shh," Karen hissed. Already the current was bearing them out, and there was a wide dark patch between boat and dock.

"Come on back."

"Can't. Current's got us."

But Hal was able to plant one oar firmly in the water and with that the boat began to turn in a slow circle.

"How was the dance?" Hal called politely.

For reply Julie stamped her foot on the dock. "Come on back," she called.

"Tell me, Julie, I sincerely want to know how it was."

"Oh, Hal, stop it."

"Actually they were very nice about it," Sid said, "but we felt kind of out of place.'

"I feel kind of out of place right here," said Jack, dizzy with the motion of the boat.

"Oh, you're all drunk," Julie said. "Every one of you is hopelessly drunk and besotted."

It ended with Sid and Julie untying another dinghy and climbing into it. Quietly then the two boats glided out with the mild current through the lighted water.

Under the lights Jack felt like an escaping prisoner caught in the beam of a spotlight, and he closed his eyes, distinctly giddy now. When he looked again, they were already emerging from the shadows of the anchored boats into the clear space beyond, where it was dark. The other boat was no longer in sight. Hal feathered the oars, and they drifted with the flow, letting Sid and Julie catch up. It was very still. They could hear Sid grunting over the oars before they saw his dinghy coming up, gaining fast. In the dark his bent over shape looked like part of the ghostly, gliding boat. Their eyes had become used to the dark by now, and they were near enough to make out ahead the narrow strip of sand edged with stunted pines that marked the shore of the island. A moment later the outline of a landing pier with several large nets spread out to dry on skeletal frames came into sight. Hal pointed the boat that way and resumed rowing.

The pier was rickety but apparently safe. When Hal leaped out, the others followed.

Karen lived with the vaguely troubling impression that someone, some man, had all her life been leaning toward her, about to touch her. It was like a dream. Instinctively she wished to draw back but could not. Moments ago, on the island, lying on the little beach, with Hal leaning toward her, whispering something about exploring the island a little farther down, around the point, she had consented without a thought, without strict attention to the words. Tomorrow, thinking back over it, excusing herself, she might suppose that she had thought Hal meant for the others to come too, but now, with that little moment still round and clear in her mind, she could admit that she had come away under no such illusion. She could not understand why she had come. Karen was not in any way angry with her husband, and she had never felt the least tremor of desire for Hal, who was simply an old friend.

Her earliest recollection of Hal was of a brash, rebellious boy in high school, a loud talker, but solitary, whom she had seen once standing alone after classes at the end of a long corridor puffing away at—strange!—a cigar, much too advanced for his years. Perhaps that was why she had been tempted to come with him now, that fragment of memory. Hal had looked up from the end of the corridor and seen her watching him puff away at the forbidden cigar, though neither had spoken at the time, nor, for that matter, had either brought the incident up since. Karen was not certain that Hal would remember it. Even if he did not, Karen believed that out of that moment, in some not-to-be-

65

explained way, this moment had come, and that it was in some way inevitable that the two of them should be standing together now, around the point from the beach where the others were lying, though not yet so far off as to keep an occasional murmur of voices from drifting their way.

Hal was no longer leaning toward her. He had taken her hand to lead her across one stretch of slippery rocks, but he had not otherwise touched her. He was talking softly and at incredible length about a book he was reading, a novel about some boys marooned on an island. Of all things! Karen thought, slightly indignant. Of all things! She had failed at the outset to catch the novelist's name, and the conversation by now was too far advanced to ask. Hal seemed to have reached the point of criticizing the style of the writer. *Seemed*—she could not really say. Her attention was failing, fading. She was overcome by a feeling of surrender, a sense of division that was almost physical, in which she stood watching herself disappear over the water, which was dark and astonishingly calm.

In the distance she could hear Sid's laughter. She had the most vivid sensation of his anxiety and of Julie's as well. She wished she might do something to alleviate it, but it was as if Hal's voice going on and on endlessly about the novel she would never read were fixing her, or a part of her, to a certain point, pinning her there, draining her of all power, while the rest of her drifted out, out . . . If only Sid would raise his voice and call her! She remembered the aftersupper games of hide-and-seek as a child with her large family of sisters and a brother. One game in particular was among her most persistent memories, one that recurred even in her dreams. She was crouching behind a prickly bush—for years afterward she could go to that same bush and point it out; she knew exactly where it stood on the lawn of her parents' house. She was the last one of all the sisters not yet found by her brother, who was "It," and she could hear her brother's footsteps coming through the dusk and then his soft voice calling, almost whispering, "Karen? Karen? Karen?" And she ran to him and threw her arms around him, whereupon her brother, who was quite a few years older and much larger than she—he was only playing the game as a favor to his sisters—lifted her from the ground and swung her around and around until they both fell to the grass, overcome with laughter and relief.

How tired she was! She wanted Hal to stop talking. She was

ready. She wanted him to touch her; she wanted whatever was going to happen to begin. Love! And yet she could not bring herself to say to him that it would be all right, that whatever he did or did not do scarcely mattered any longer.

Jack woke from a sound sleep feeling cold. He was alone.

He sat up and listened, a little apprehensively, for some sound to indicate where the others might be. Except for the water that was licking up along the sand almost to his feet and out again, the silence was complete. Where had they gone? He took it for granted that they were off exploring the island, two by two probably, but by what pairs and for what purpose he hardly considered. His curiosity, brimming not long before, had gone flat.

Somewhere he had misplaced his glasses. Groping in the sand near where he had been sleeping, failing to find them, he blinked out across the water into the sky. The first faint streaks and patches of light were beginning to show. For a long time he sat, reluctant to get up and start looking for the others. He did not like the idea of stumbling across them in the dark, especially half-blind as he was. For the time being he did not care if he never saw any of them again. His stomach felt a little queasy, but he was not sure if it was from drinking. It might have been from emotion. In any case, he had been through worse.

Only after he had made his way back along the path to the landing pier and seen that the boats were missing did he realize what had happened. They had left him behind; they had abandoned him on the island.

At first he was simply angry. He peered as well as he could toward land. The sailing-club lights were still burning over the water. That he could see, but no farther. It was beginning to get light, and soon, he knew, the night watchman would wake up and turn the lights off. Already the lights were beginning to look superfluous. What a stupid joke this was, he thought. He imagined the story they would make out of it—the night they marooned Jack on the island! For a moment he considered the chance of swimming back, like Roberta. If he could make seventy or eighty yards on his own, there would be plenty of boats to hang on to. But the water looked cold, and his stomach was too unsettled.

Cold after the warmth of the night, he wrapped his arms

around his shoulders. He felt as alone as he could ever remember having felt, and in an unfamiliar place, a place he could not even, without his glasses, see clearly, all fuzzy and vague—the last absurd touch. Any minute his teeth would start chattering. Standing there like that, realizing how foolish and pointless it was, for he must have been very nearly sober by then, he began to call their names out as loud as he could, one after the other —a kind of roll call—whether out of annoyance or affection he did not pause to consider. *Hal, Sid, Karen, Julie!* He had no idea how far his voice carried over the water, and in any case there was no answer.

At last he sat down on the little rickety pier and began to wait for someone to come and rescue him. And gradually, sitting there, beginning to shiver with the morning cool, Jack reflected, absurdly enough, that he was to be the hero of whatever story came to be told of the night. A curious form of flattery, but flattery of a sort. He had been singled out. At once he felt better about the evening. The party—it had not been a dead loss, after all. He almost found himself forgiving them for having abandoned him; eventually perhaps he would forgive them, forgive them everything, whatever they had done or not done. Without him, whatever had happened—and he did not want to know yet what that was, afraid that his new and still fragile sense of the uniqueness of the evening might evaporate once he knew—would not have happened. In some way, he was responsible. In any case, he would have forgiven them a great deal—laughter, humiliation, even perhaps betrayal—as they would forgive him practically anything. He saw all that now. Well, it was a sentimental time of night—the very end of it—and he had had a lot to drink, but he was willing to believe that the future would indeed be bleak and awful without such friends, willing to take their chance with you, ready even to abandon you on a chunk of sand at four A.M. for nothing but the sheer hell of it. And he was, for the moment, remarkably contented.

Brighton, 1980

The apartment building the Langs had lived in had been gone since the late sixties. There had been a boom. The fine old house—one of the oldest in the area, one to which Indians just before the turn of the century had come up across the bay in their canoes to trade—had lasted as long as any, but it had succumbed in the end to time and money. In any case, it would have been quickly dwarfed by the new high-rises looming around it. On its site stood one of the poshest of the latest generation of high-rises, expensive and grand, with glass and impractical little tilted balconies painted in three bold colors. Admittedly, it had been and was still a grand site, with a marvellous sweeping view of the bay, the little masted boats thick on the water, like blown leaves.

But it was the people who concerned Jack. And he knew none of the new people. In his own place, when he went there now, he felt uncomfortable and alien.

One day—twenty years and more had passed—sitting in a flat in Brighton, England, looking idly out over the gray, disturbed sea in a direction he thought must be toward home, Jack began making a sort of mental catalogue of all his friends from that period. He had not thought it out in advance. The idea just came to him, and he began. He was trying to remember everyone who was together at a certain time in the old life, at a precise moment even, and the night of his going-away party came back to him.

The list began with Susan's son, the one she had been pregnant with at the time, and Jack was pleased with himself for having thought to include her child-to-be in his recollection. She never had another. The son, he had heard, was a fine, intelligent boy, off at college somewhere, no trouble to anybody. Jack had not seen him since the boy started grammar school. The boy's name slipped his memory, but he did remember, if not very clearly, curls and a sort of general shying away from the presence of grownups.

The sallow husband—Robert or Bob—had been some trouble or had some trouble. Drinking? Whatever in the past had caused his silence, he was to sink deeper and deeper into it over the years. Eventually he had found his way back north to Philadelphia, into his father's business, a chain of liquor stores. Just the thing, Jack thought ruefully, just the thing.

Susan herself was another story, though not much of one. She owned a small stucco house in the Grove, almost hidden by shrubs and palms and jacarandas. Her time seemed to go into nothing at all, unless it was a little gardening, but it surely went. She had no time for anything, certainly not for friends, and never or very rarely ventured out. She kept a few cats, quite a few. Their number grew.

The great surprise was Sid, the only one to have become famous. Not exactly famous, Jack acknowledged, but well-known. No one had sensed the power and ambition hidden so quietly in Sid back then, certainly not Karen. From small starts, from short sailing trips down into the Keys, later out to the Bahamas, Sid had taken the great dare of a long solo sail across the Atlantic, kept a journal, and published an account of the voyage. Modestly popular. Later, other adventures, other books. He was married now to a minor movie actress, past her prime but still quite beautiful—a brunette, not at all like Karen in appearance—and they lived most of the year, predictably some-how, in southern France. (It was true—his family had had some money.) Jack had recently had occasion to call on them on the continent and found that he enjoyed his visit immensely. Sid had become voluble, a great smiler—of all of them, the most thoroughly and happily changed.

Karen, on the other hand, had been through three more husbands. Two daughters, one of them married, with a daugh-ter of her own. It seemed incredible to Jack that Karen, of all people, should have become a grandmother. It was like a magic trick, seen but not believed. Sometimes, of an evening, as they sat talking over a drink beside the current husband's pool, the bug light sending out its intermittent little zap, he had caught a sidelong glimpse of the former Karen, a Karen absolute and undiminished, still slender, seemingly remote, cool if not cold, not to be found out. Some secret she had, and it had kept her beautiful. Her present husband was often ill, and there was a bad look around her own eyes. She looked away from you much of the time. She had never done anything of any importance in her life, and everybody had always loved her for herself alone. What happiness!

Julie, as she had wished, never had had any children. Over the years she had gone a little to corpulence, but her foot, sur-prisingly tiny still, still swung back and forth to some nervous rhythm of her own. She, who had always abhorred and fled from the cold, ran a bookstore now in Boston. She had become an ex-pert on books. The way Jack had of explaining this to himself— he had browsed in her shop once or twice when in the city—was simply that she had liked to read, always. Those nights Hal had been out catting around she had read. She had read and read and she had always loved books and, in the end, it had come to this. She seemed satisfied.

Nor was Hal—the great romantic, Hal—a totally lost cause, even though he had, in his maturity, held down a steady job, the same job now, for ten or eleven years, easily a record for him. He managed a gallery. He was perfect for it, a gallery in the Grove popular with everyone, wealthy tourists especially. It also provided him the contacts with women he seemed to need—wives, daughters, perhaps even a youthful grandmother or two. Women, young and old, some beautiful, some rich, pursuing Hal, who was not getting any younger. He let his colorful shirts hang out usually, over a slight belly, wore dark glasses much of the time, rode out his hangovers with good grace and considerable experience. He still painted, excellent miniatures, obsessively detailed, with the clear jeweled colors of Byzantine work. He sold everything he made and never set too high a price, though it was certain he could demand more if he chose. But no, he was as happy as he deserved, perhaps happier. Not married—it was easier that way. Some nights he liked being alone.

Several of his friends, Jack realized, were actually happy. The shape of their futures must always have been there, somehow, just as eye color is built into the chromosomes before birth. Impossible to read, all the same, except backward, as with some obscure Eastern language. Or perhaps the night of the party had been a sort of key, and it had been clear, or should have been clear then, that the Langs would never last, not as a couple, and if the Langs went, then the Greens constituted a doubtful case; and something in the way her husband had cast his silent, wary, unfathomable glances at the pregnant Susan might have hinted at some future division between them as well. Now no one was married to the right person. No one, as Jack would have it, would ever be married to the right person again. The time when everything was as it should be was always really some other time, but back then, that summer, it had seemed near.

From the window of the flat he could see only a little corner of the sea, and he wanted, for some reason, to be closer to the water. Dressing warmly, Jack walked down to the parade, braced himself against the baby gale and walked and walked, for forty minutes or so. He found himself down on the shingle, almost alone there. It was too nasty a day for there to be much company. A big boat hung on the horizon. Jack thought back to the beach of the little sandy bay island and he guessed that what had happened that night must be why he had ventured down to the sand now, to which he almost never descended. Here in this foreign place he felt again that he was on a little island, isolated, the last civilized speck, himself against a faceless and unpredictable world—unknowable, really. Jack felt like calling out the names again, the names of his friends, but of course he did not. He could not even remember how he had been rescued that other time, who it was that had come out in a dinghy for him, risking the wrath of the sleepy night watchman. Probably Sid. Julie had cooked a nice breakfast—he remembered that. No one would be coming to rescue him now, not that he needed rescuing or wanted rescuing, even in the sort of half-dreaming state he had fallen into. But the thought did occur to him, in passing.

Notes

Nineteenth Century Portrait. See Baudelaire's "*A une Mala-baraise.*" I have shifted the scene from Malabar and Paris to the Caribbean and New York. Richard Howard's translation provided the hibiscus.

American Scenes (1904–1905). The first section is pieced together from the *Notebooks*, the second and third sections from *American Scenes*. In California James stayed at the famous Hotel del Coronado near San Diego.

Young Girls Growing Up (1911). See *The Diaries of Franz Kafka: 1910–1913*, entries for November 29 and December 3.

Both Rilke poems date from the poet's stay in Capri during the first part of 1907. My versions came out of an attempt to write a play based loosely on that period in Rilke's life. The famous image of the death's-head shako with which "*Letzer Abend*" ends I have dePrussianized, since in my play both poet and setting had become American. See "*Lied vom Meer (Capri, Piccola Marina)*" and "*Letzer Abend.*"

Purgatory. Line 4 is taken unchanged from "The Spell," a poem in Robert Boardman Vaughn's unpublished ms. Parts of the next few lines are from his "The Black Robe," but have been altered.

The Sunset Maker and *Little Elegy for Cello and Piano.* The musical quotation comes from a piece I composed for Carl Ruggles in 1943.

Donald Justice was born in Miami, Florida, in 1925 and grew up there. After graduating from the University of Miami, where he had studied musical composition with Carl Ruggles, he attended the University of North Carolina, Stanford, and Iowa. He has taught at a number of universities, including Syracuse and Iowa, as well as the University of Florida, where he now teaches, having returned to his native state in 1982. His first book, *The Summer Anniversaries*, was the Lamont Poetry Selection for 1959. It was followed by *Night Light* (1967), *Departures* (1973), and *Selected Poems* (1979), which the following year was awarded the Pulitzer Prize in poetry. He has also edited *The Collected Poems of Weldon Kees* (1960). He has received grants in poetry from The Rockefeller Foundation, The Guggenheim Foundation, and the National Endowment for the Arts. He and his wife, Jean Ross, have one son, Nathaniel.